MEG at SEA

for Hannah

MEG at SEA

by Helen Nicoll
and Jan Pieńkowski

PUFFIN BOOKS

Meg, Mog and Owl

went to
the seaside

They went out in a boat

but there was no wind

The wind blew

A storm blew up

and they swam to land

It
was
an
island

They were cold,

wet and hungry

Mog and Owl
went
fishing

They took the fish to Meg

Mog cooked the fish

Meg
made
smoke
signals
with
her
cloak

The helicopter saw them

and took them back home

Goodbye!